MACBETH

WILLIAM SHAKESPEARE

www.realreads.co.uk

Illu

ng

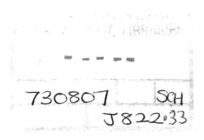

Published by Real Reads Ltd
Stroud, Gloucestershire, UK
www.realreads.co.uk

First published in 2010

ISBN 978-1-906230-47-0

Printed in China by Imago Ltd
Designed by Lucy Guenot
Typeset by Bookcraft Ltd, Stroud, Gloucestershire

CONTENTS

THE CHARACTERS

Macbeth and Lady Macbeth

Everything goes well for this successful pair, until they start craving more power, fame and riches. Will Macbeth stop at nothing to get what he wants?

Banquo and Fleance

Banquo is Macbeth's friend, but is that enough to keep him and his son, Fleance, safe?

Macduff

This Scottish lord is not easily taken in by the new king. What secret does he hold that could be Macbeth's undoing?

Duncan, Malcolm and Donalbain

Duncan is the King of Scotland – until he goes to stay with the Macbeths. Will Duncan's sons, Malcolm and Donalbain, escape their father's fate?

The Witches

What the three witches tell Macbeth about his future sounds too good to be true. Should he believe what they say?

Lennox and Ross

These two Scottish lords find their loyalties divided between the new king and the man they consider the rightful king. Which should they choose?

MACBETH

ACT ONE, SCENE ONE
A DESERT HEATH

First witch

When shall we three meet again
In thunder, lightning, or in rain?

Second witch

When the hurlyburly's done,
When the battle's lost or won.

Third witch

That will be ere the set of sun.

First witch

Where the place?

Second witch

Upon the heath.

Third witch

There to meet with Macbeth.

All three witches

Fair is foul, and foul is fair;
Hover through the fog and filthy air.

The witches leave.

Duncan, King of Scotland, and his son, Malcolm,
enter and meet a soldier.

Duncan

What bloody man is that? His open wounds
Do show he comes fresh from the battlefield.

Malcolm

This is the sergeant,
Who like a good and hardy soldier fought
'Gainst my captivity. Hail brave friend!
Say to the King, the knowledge of the fight
As thou didst leave it.

Captain

Doubtful it stood, then did brave Macbeth
(He well deserves that name) carve out a path
With fiery sword towards the rebel fiend.
Then was the merciless Macdonald slain.
His head is now upon our battlements!

Duncan

O valiant cousin! Worthy Macbeth!

Captain

And yet no sooner was this victory won
But Norway's king began a fresh assault.

Duncan

Dismayed not this
Our captains, Macbeth and Banquo?

Captain

In as much as sparrows frighten eagles!
But I am faint. My gashes cry for help.

Duncan

Thou hast done well. Take him to a surgeon.

Ross enters.

Malcolm

The worthy Thane of Ross.

Duncan

What news?

Ross

The vast Norwegian army and their king,
Assisted by that most disloyal traitor
The Thane of Cawdor, bore down upon our men.
But fearless, brave Macbeth confronted them
And, to conclude, the victory fell on us.

Duncan

The Thane of Cawdor shall be put to death
And, with his former title, greet Macbeth.

Ross

I'll see it done.

Duncan

What he hath lost, noble Macbeth hath won.

Ross, Duncan and Malcolm leave.
The three witches enter.

Witches

A drum! A drum! Macbeth doth come.

Macbeth and Banquo enter.

Banquo

How far is it to Forres? What are these,
So wither'd, and so wild in their attire?

Macbeth

Speak if you can: what are you?

First witch

All hail Macbeth!
Hail to thee, Thane of Glamis!

Second witch

All hail Macbeth!
Hail to thee, Thane of Cawdor!

Third witch

All hail Macbeth, that shalt be king hereafter!

Banquo

You greet my noble friend with great predictions.
If you can look into the seeds of time,
And say which grain will grow, and which will not,
Speak then to me, who neither beg, nor fear
Your favours, nor your hate.

All three witches

Hail! Hail! Hail!

First witch

Lesser than Macbeth, and greater.

Second witch

Not so happy, yet much happier.

Third witch

Thou shalt get kings, though thou be none.
So all hail Macbeth, and Banquo.

Macbeth

Stay, you imperfect speakers, tell me more.
By Sinel's death, I know I am Thane of Glamis,
But how of Cawdor? The Thane of Cawdor lives,
And to be king stands not within belief.

The witches vanish.

Banquo
The earth hath bubbles, as the water has,
And these are of them. Whither are they vanished?

Macbeth
To air. Melted, as breath into the wind.
Your children shall be kings.

Banquo
You shall be king.

Macbeth
And Thane of Cawdor, too – went it not so?

Banquo
Those very words, my friend. But who comes here?

Ross enters.

Ross

The King has heard the happy news, Macbeth,

Of your success, and as reward for this

He bade me, from him, call thee Thane of Cawdor.

Macbeth

The Thane of Cawdor lives.

Why do you dress me in borrowed robes?

Ross

Who was the Thane lives yet,

But soon will lose his life for treachery.

Macbeth *(to Ross)*

Thanks for your pains.

(to Banquo)

Do you not hope your children shall be kings,

When those that gave the Thane of Cawdor to me

Promised no less to them?

Banquo

They also promised you the crown. Sometimes

The instruments of darkness tell us truths,

Win us with honest trifles, then trick us

In more important things.

Macbeth *(to himself)*
Two truths are told, and so why not the third?
These supernatural messages I think
Cannot be ill; cannot be good.
If ill, why am I then Thane of Cawdor?
If good, why do I think this evil thought
Whose horrid image doth unfix my hair
And make my seated heart knock at my ribs?

Banquo
Look how our partner's lost in thought.

Macbeth *(to himself)*
If fate will have me king, then fate may crown me
Without the need for me to do the deed.

ACT ONE, SCENE TWO
ELSEWHERE ON THE HEATH

Duncan
Is execution done on Cawdor?

Malcolm
It is, my liege.

Macbeth and Banquo enter.

Duncan

Worthy Macbeth! My thanks are not enough
For all that you have done for me. Welcome.

Macbeth

Your highness, duty has its own reward.

Duncan

And noble Banquo, no less deserving.
Let me embrace thee. Now the war is won,
I wish you all to know that my dear son,
My eldest, Malcolm, shall be my rightful heir.
And now, Macbeth, we will to Inverness
To stay with you and make our friendship strong.

Macbeth

I'll send a joyful message to my wife
Of your approach, and ride ahead of you
To make the preparations for your stay.
I humbly take my leave.
(to himself)
Malcolm shall be his heir; that is a step
On which I must fall down, or else o'erleap,
For in my way it lies. Stars, hide your fires;
Let not light see my black and deep desires.

ACT TWO, SCENE ONE
MACBETH'S CASTLE AT INVERNESS

Lady Macbeth enters, reading a letter.

Lady Macbeth

'They met me in the day of victory, and I am
sure they were not of this world, for when I
questioned them further they vanished into the
air. Then messengers from the King declared
me Thane of Cawdor, by which title the weird
sisters had hailed me earlier, as well as king that
shall be. This have I thought good to share with
you. Lay it to thy heart, and farewell.'
Glamis thou art, and Cawdor, and shalt be
What thou art promised; yet do I fear thy nature.
It is too full of the milk of human kindness.
Make haste to me that I may make thee bold
To grasp this crown that has been offered thee.

A messenger enters.

Messenger

The King comes here tonight.

Lady Macbeth

You bring great news.

The messenger leaves.

The raven himself is hoarse
That croaks the fatal entrance of Duncan
Under my battlements. Then come, thick night,
And hide thee in the blackest smoke of hell,
That my keen knife sees not the wound it makes,
Nor heaven peep through blanket of the dark
To cry, 'Hold, hold'.

Macbeth

If we decide to do this dreadful deed

It must be swiftly done to have success.

And yet the things we do sometimes come back

To punish us. He's here in double trust.

First, I am his kinsman and his subject.

Secondly, I am his host; my part

Should be to keep him safe from villainy,

Not bear the knife myself.

Lady Macbeth enters.

How now? What news?

Lady Macbeth

He has almost supp'd. Why have you left the chamber?

Macbeth

Hath he asked for me?

Lady Macbeth

Know you not he has?

Macbeth

We will proceed no further in this business.

Lady Macbeth

Has boldness turned to cowardice in you?

Macbeth

Prithee, peace, I dare do all that may become a man.

Lady Macbeth
When you durst do it, then you were a man.

Macbeth
If we should fail?

Lady Macbeth
But we'll not fail. When Duncan is asleep,
I will his guards with so much wine make drunk
That they will sleep as soundly as the dead.
What cannot you and I perform upon
The unguarded Duncan?

Macbeth
                                    O, spirited
And fearless wife! Will it not be believed
When we have marked with blood those sleepy two
Of his own chamber, and used their very daggers,
That they have done it?

Lady Macbeth
                                    It will, my dearest,
For we'll lament and weep with all the rest
Upon his death.

Macbeth
                        I am settled. But now
Away, and mock the time with fairest show,
False face must hide what the false heart doth know.

ACT TWO, SCENE THREE
INVERNESS CASTLE

Macbeth *(to servant)*

Go bid thy mistress, when my drink is ready,

She strike upon the bell. Get thee to bed.

The servant leaves.

Is this a dagger which I see before me,

Handle toward my hand? Come, let me clutch thee.

I have thee not, and yet I see thee still.

Art thou real and solid, or art thou but

A dagger of the mind, a false creation?

Thou point'st towards the way that I was going,

And on thy blade and handle drops of blood

Which was not so before. There's no such thing.

This bloody business does play tricks on me.

A bell rings.

I go, and it is done: the bell invites me.

Hear it not, Duncan, for it is a knell

That summons thee to heaven, or to hell.

Macbeth leaves.

Lady Macbeth

That which hath made them drunk hath made me bold;

What hath quenched them hath given me fire.

Hark! Peace! It was the owl that shrieked.

Alack, I am afraid they have awaked,

And 'tis not done. I laid their daggers ready;

He could not miss them. Had he not resembled

My father as he slept, I'd have done it.

Macbeth enters.

Macbeth

I have done the deed. Didst thou not hear a noise?

Lady Macbeth

I heard the owl scream and the crickets cry.

Macbeth

Methought I heard a voice cry, 'Sleep no more:

Glamis hath murdered sleep, and therefore Cawdor

Shall sleep no more; Macbeth shall sleep no more.'

Lady Macbeth

O, worthy thane, you do upset your mind

To think these thoughts. Go get some water,

And wash this filthy witness from your hand.

Why did you bring these daggers from the place?

They must lie there: go carry them, and smear
The sleepy grooms with blood.

Macbeth
                              I'll go no more;
I am afraid to think what I have done.
Look on it again I dare not.

Lady Macbeth
                         You coward!
Give me the daggers. If he do bleed,
I'll daub the faces of the grooms with it,
For it must seem their guilt.

She leaves with the daggers.

Macbeth
These hands! I cannot bear to look on them.
Will all great Neptune's ocean wash this blood
Clean from my hand? No, rather will my hand
The waters stain, making the green sea red.

Lady Macbeth returns with blood on her hands.

Lady Macbeth
My hands are of your colour, but I shame
To wear a heart so white.

Knocking is heard.

I hear a knocking at the south entry.
Retire we to our chamber;
A little water clears us of this deed.

ACT TWO, SCENE FIVE
INVERNESS CASTLE

Macduff
Is the master stirring?
Our knocking has awaked him: here he comes.

Macbeth enters.

Lennox
Good morrow, noble sir.

Macbeth
Good morrow both.

Macduff
Is the King stirring, worthy thane?

Macbeth
Not yet.

Macduff
He did command me to call timely on him:
I have almost slipped the hour.

Macbeth
I'll bring you to him. This is the door.

Macduff leaves.

23

Lennox

The night has been unruly. Where we lay
Our chimneys were blown down, and (as they say)
Lamentings heard in the air; strange screams of death.
Some say the earth was feverous and did shake.

Macbeth

'Twas a rough night.

Macduff comes back.

Macduff

O horror! Horror! Horror!
Tongue nor heart cannot conceive, nor name thee.
Most cruel and bloody murder has stolen
The very life of our most precious lord.

Lennox

Mean you his majesty?

Macduff

Approach the chamber, and look upon it,
But do not bid me say what I have seen.

Macbeth and Lennox leave.

Ring the alarum bell: murder, and treason.
Banquo and Donalbain, Malcolm, awake!
As from your graves rise up. Sound the alarm!

Lady Macbeth enters.

Lady Macbeth
What is the meaning of this commotion
That wakes the sleepers of the house? Speak.

Macduff
O gentle lady,
'Tis not for you to hear what I can speak.

Banquo enters.

O Banquo, Banquo, our royal master's murdered.

Lady Macbeth
Woe, alas! What, in our house?

Banquo

Dear Duff, I prithee contradict thyself,
And say it is not so.

Macbeth and Lennox enter.

Macbeth

Had I but died an hour before this time
I had lived a blessed life.

Malcolm and Donalbain enter.

Malcolm

What is amiss?

Macduff

Your royal father's murdered.

Malcolm

By whom?

Lennox

Those of his chamber, as it seemed, had done it.

Macbeth

O, yet I do repent me of my fury,
That I did kill them.

Macduff

Wherefore did you so?

Macbeth

O, who could blame me? For there lay Duncan,
His silver skin laced with his golden blood
That poured from out such piteous wounds.
My love for him cried out aloud for vengeance.

Lady Macbeth

Help me! *(She faints)*

Banquo

Look to the lady!
Let's quickly dress and in the hall we'll meet,
To question this most bloody piece of work.

All

Agreed.

All leave except Malcolm and Donalbain.

Malcolm

I do not trust these men. There could be worse
To come. What will you do? I'll to England.

Donalbain

To Ireland I. Separate ways are safer.
Where we are, there's daggers in men's smiles.

ACT TWO, SCENE SIX
OUTSIDE INVERNESS CASTLE

Ross

Here comes the good Macduff.

How goes the world, sir, now?

Macduff

Why, see you not?

Ross

Is't known who did this more than bloody deed?

Macduff

Malcolm and Donalbain, the King's two sons
Have fled away, which puts upon them both
Suspicion of the deed.

Ross

                        Then 'tis most like
The sovereignty will fall upon Macbeth.

Macduff

He is already named and gone to Scone
To be invested.

Ross

                Will you to Scone?

Macduff

No, cousin, I'll to Fife. Who knows how well
Or ill may prove this newest state of things.

ACT THREE, SCENE ONE
THE COURT AT INVERNESS CASTLE

Banquo *(to himself)*
Thou hast it now: King, Cawdor, Glamis, all,
As the weird women promised, and I fear
Thou played most foully for it. Yet 'twas said
That I, not thou, should be the ancestor
Of many kings. If there come truth from them,
As upon thee, Macbeth, their speeches shine
And set me up in hope. But hush, no more.

Macbeth and Lady Macbeth enter as king and queen,
accompanied by servants.

Lady Macbeth *(gesturing to Banquo)*
Here's our chief guest.

Macbeth

If he had been forgotten,

It had been as a gap in our feast.

Lady Macbeth

Tonight we hold a solemn supper, sir,

And I'll request your presence.

Banquo

As your highness wishes.

Macbeth

Let everyone be master of his time.

We'll keep ourself till supper-time alone.

All leave except Macbeth and a servant.

Some men are by the gate. Bring them to me.

The servant leaves.

I'm king, but for how long will that remain?

Our fears in Banquo stick deep. The sisters

Did hail him father to a line of kings;

Upon my head they placed a fruitless crown.

His sons, not mine, shall have this throne from me;

For them the gracious Duncan have I killed.

Two murderers enter.

Was it not yesterday we spoke together?

First murderer

It was, so please your highness.

Macbeth
You know that Banquo is your enemy.

Second murderer
We do, my lord.

Macbeth
So is he mine. And in your hands I place
The task of ridding me of him.
It must be done tonight away from here.
Fleance, his son, must also die. Now go.

The murderers leave. Lady Macbeth enters.

Lady Macbeth
How now, my lord, why do you keep alone?
Don't dwell on troubled thoughts. What's done is done.

Macbeth
Good Duncan is at peace and in his grave.
After life's fitful fever he sleeps well;
While we lie tossed in these terrible dreams
That shake us nightly.
O, full of scorpions is my mind, dear wife.

Lady Macbeth
Gentle my lord, sleek o'er your rugged looks,
Be bright and jovial among your guests tonight.

Macbeth
So shall I, love, and so I pray be you.

ACT THREE, SCENE TWO
THE CASTLE'S BANQUET HALL

Macbeth

There's blood upon thy face.

Murderer

'Tis Banquo's then.

My lord, his throat is cut, that I did for him.

Macbeth

And did you do the same for Fleance?

Murderer

Most royal sir, Fleance is fled.

Macbeth

This vexes me! But go, we'll speak again.

*The murderer leaves. Lennox, Ross, Lady Macbeth
and others enter for the feast.*

Macbeth

Welcome, gentlemen. Sit down.

All

Your majesty!

Banquo's ghost appears and sits in Macbeth's place.

Macbeth

'Tis pity noble Banquo is not here.

Ross

He breaks his promise to attend; but sire,
Please grace us with your royal company.

Macbeth

The table's full.

Lennox

Here is a place reserved, sir.

Macbeth

Where?

Lennox

Here, my good lord.

Macbeth sees Banquo's ghost.

What moves your highness?

Macbeth

Thou canst not say I did it. Never shake
Thy gory locks at me.

Ross

Gentlemen, rise, his highness is not well.

Lady Macbeth

Sit, worthy friends: my lord is often thus,
And hath been since his youth. Pray you keep seat.
(to Macbeth)
Why do you make such faces? When all's done
You look but on a stool.

Macbeth

Prithee see there!

The ghost disappears.

If I stand here, I saw him.

Lady Macbeth *(to Macbeth)*

Fie for shame. This is the very painting of your fear.

This is the air-drawn dagger which, you said,

Led you to Duncan.

(to all)

My worthy lord, your noble friends do lack you.

Macbeth *(to all)*

I have a strange infirmity, which is nothing

To those that know me. Come, love and health to all,

Then I'll sit down. Give me some wine, fill full.

I drink to the general joy of the whole table,

And to our dear friend, Banquo, whom we miss.

Would he were here! To all, and him, we drink.

All
Our duties, and the pledge.

The ghost reappear.

Macbeth
Avaunt and quit my sight, let the earth hide thee.
Thy bones are marrowless, thy blood is cold.
Hence, horrible shadow, hence.

The ghost disappears.

Lady Macbeth *(to Macbeth)*
You have displaced the mirth,

(to all)
I pray you, speak not, he grows worse and worse.
Stand not upon the order of your going,
But go at once.

Lennox
Goodnight, and better health attend his majesty.

Lady Macbeth
A kind goodnight to all.

All but Macbeth and Lady Macbeth leave.

Macbeth
I am in blood
Stepped in so far that should I wade no more.
Returning were as tedious as going o'er.

ACT FOUR, SCENE ONE
THE HEATH

The witches stand around a cauldron.

First witch
The spirits cry: 'tis time, 'tis time.
Round about the cauldron go,
In the poisoned entrails throw.

All the witches
Double, double toil and trouble;
Fire burn, and cauldron bubble.

Second witch

Eye of newt, and toe of frog,

Wool of bat, and tongue of dog.

Third witch

Adder's fork, and blind-worm's sting,

Lizard's leg, and howlet's wing.

First witch

For a charm of powerful trouble,

Like a hell-broth, boil and bubble.

All the witches

Double, double toil and trouble,

Fire burn, and cauldron bubble.

First witch

By the pricking of my thumbs,

Something wicked this way comes.

Macbeth enters.

Macbeth

How now you secret, black, and midnight hags,

What is't you do?

All the witches

A deed without a name.

Macbeth

I conjure you to answer what I ask.

First witch

Speak.

Second witch

Demand.

Third witch

We'll answer.

All the witches

We call you, masters, your powers now show
All that wicked Macbeth would know.

Three apparitions appear.

First apparition

Macbeth, Macbeth, Macbeth.
Beware Macduff, beware the Thane of Fife.

Macbeth

Whate'er thou art, for thy good caution, thanks.

Second apparition

Be bloody, bold, and resolute; laugh to scorn
The power of man, for none of woman born
Shall harm Macbeth.

Macbeth

Then live Macduff, what need I fear of thee?
But yet, I must be sure. Thou shalt not live.

Third apparition

Macbeth shall never vanquished be until
Great Birnam Wood to high Dunsinane Hill
Shall come against him.

Macbeth

That will never be;
Who can command the forest, bid the tree
Unfix his earth-bound root? Yet my heart
Throbs to know: shall Banquo's children ever
Reign in this kingdom?

All the witches

Seek to know no more.

Macbeth

I will be satisfied. Deny me this
And an eternal curse fall on you. Let me know.

All the witches

Show his eyes and grieve his heart,
Come like shadows, so depart.

The witches disappear as Banquo and a line of kings appear.

Macbeth

What? Will the line stretch out to the crack of doom?

Horrible sight, now I see 'tis true,

The blood-spattered Banquo smiles upon me

And points at them, for they are his. 'Tis so.

The apparitions vanish, and Lennox enters.

Lennox

Macduff is fled to England.

Macbeth

Fled to England?

Lennox

Ay, my good lord.

Macbeth *(to himself)*

The castle of Macduff I will surprise,

Seize upon Fife, put to death his wife,

His babes, and all unfortunate souls

That trace him in his line. This deed I'll do.

ACT FOUR, SCENE TWO
AT THE ENGLISH COURT

Macduff

Sire, we have need of you to be our king
And march with us against Macbeth.

Malcolm

Though I am young and inexperienced,
Myself at my poor country's service lay.
Old Siward with ten thousand Englishmen
Is setting forth to bring the tyrant down,
So shall we ride to free our countrymen.

Ross enters.

Macduff

My ever gentle cousin, welcome hither.
What news from Scotland?

Ross

Let not your ears despise my tongue forever.

Macduff

Speak.

Ross

Your castle is surprised, your wife and babes
Savagely slaughtered.

Malcolm
Merciful heavens!

Macduff
My children too?

Ross
Wife, children, servants, all that could be found.

Macduff
Sinful Macduff, they were all struck for thee.

Malcolm
Be this the whetstone of your sword; let grief
Convert to anger. Blunt not the heart, enrage it!

Macduff
O bring this fiend of Scotland before me,
Within sword's length, then will he know my grief.

Malcolm
The time has come, our soldiers are now ready.
Come, go we to the King and take our leave.

43

ACT FIVE, SCENE ONE
AT DUNSINANE CASTLE

Lady-in-waiting

I have seen her, sir, rise from her bed,

And, at her table, write while still asleep.

Doctor

And does she speak while thus?

Lady-in-waiting

She does. But what she says I shall repeat to no one.

But lo, she comes. Her eyes are open

But she is fast asleep, I swear.

Lady Macbeth

Out damned spot, out I say!
Yet who would have thought the old man
To have so much blood in him?

Lady-in-waiting

Did you hear that?

Lady Macbeth

The Thane of Fife had a wife. Where is she now?
What, will these hands ne'er be clean?

Doctor

She has spoke what she should not.

Lady Macbeth

Wash your hands, put on your nightgown; look not so pale.
I tell you yet again, Banquo's buried:
He cannot come out of his grave.
What's done cannot be undone. To bed, to bed, to bed.

Lady Macbeth leaves.

Doctor

I can do nothing for her. Look after her
And still keep eyes upon her.

Lady-in-waiting

Good night, good doctor.

ACT FIVE, SCENE TWO
THE COUNTRY NEAR DUNSINANE

Lennox enters, with some other Scottish lords.

First lord

The English power is near, led on by Malcolm,
His uncle Siward, and the good Macduff.

Second lord

Near Birnam Wood shall we meet with them
And join their ranks to march against Macbeth.

First lord

What does the tyrant?

Lennox

Great Dunsinane he strongly fortifies;
Some say he's mad.

Second lord

          Now does he feel
The secret murders sticking on his hands.
Now does he feel his title hang loose about him,
Like a giant's robe upon a dwarfish thief.

Lennox

Well, march we on
To give obedience to where 'tis truly owed.

ACT FIVE, SCENE THREE
DUNSINANE CASTLE

Macbeth and a servant enter.

Macbeth

Bring me no more reports, let them fly all.
Till Birnam Wood remove to Dunsinane
I shall not be afraid. What's the boy Malcolm?
Was he not born of woman? Fly, false thanes,
And join the English force to do your worst.

Servant

There are ten thousand, sire!

Macbeth

I'll fight till from my bones my flesh be hacked.
Send out more horses, skirt the country round,
Hang those that talk of fear! Give me my armour!

ACT FIVE, SCENE FOUR
BIRNAM WOOD

Malcolm, Macduff, Lennox and the Scottish lords meet.

Malcolm
What wood is this before us?

Lennox
The wood of Birnam.

Malcolm
Let every soldier cut him down a bough
And carry it before him; thereby
Shall we disguise the number of our force.

Lords
It shall be done.

Macduff
The tyrant stays in Dunsinane and waits
For us to come to him.

Lennox
He has no choice.
So many have deserted him that now
His soldiers stay from fear of him, not love.

ACT FIVE, SCENE FIVE
DUNSINANE CASTLE

Macbeth

Hang out our banners on the outward walls;
Our castle's strength will laugh a siege to scorn.

A cry of women is heard.

What cry is that?

A servant enters.

Servant

The queen, my lord, is dead.

Macbeth

If she had died some other time but now
There would have been a time to speak our grief.
Out, out, brief candle.
Life's but a walking shadow, a poor player
That struts and frets his hour upon the stage,
And then is heard no more.

A messenger enters.

Thou com'st to use thy tongue: thy story quickly!

Messenger

As I did stand my watch upon the hill
I looked toward Birnam, and soon I thought
The wood began to move.

Macbeth

Liar!

Messenger

Let me endure your wrath if it be not so.

Within this three mile you may see it coming.

Macbeth

If thou speakest false, upon the next tree

Shalt thou hang alive. But if it be true

So is the prophecy fulfilled: fear not

Till Birnam Wood do come to Dunsinane.

And now a wood does come against me.

Take up your weapons. To battle go,

There is no point in staying here to die,

For I've begun to weary of this life.

Ring the alarm bell! Blow, wind! Come, wrack!

At least we'll die with armour on our back.

ACT FIVE, SCENE SIX
THE BATTLEFIELD

Macbeth

They have me trapped, I cannot fly from here.
Then I must stay and fight. Who could it be
That was not born of woman? He's the one
That I should fear, or none at all.

Siward's son enters.

Young Siward
Thy name?

Macbeth
Thou'lt be afraid to hear it.

Young Siward
I doubt that could be so.

Macbeth
My name's Macbeth.

Young Siward
The devil himself could not pronounce a name
More hateful to my ear.

They fight, and Macbeth kills young Siward.

Macbeth
Thou wast born of woman.

Macduff enters.

Macduff

Turn hell-hound, turn!

Macbeth

Of all men else I have avoided thee,

But get thee back. My soul is too much charged

With blood of thine already.

Macduff

I have no words, my voice is in my sword.

They fight.

Macbeth

You waste your time and strength on me, Macduff.

'Tis easier to wound the swirling air

With thy sharp sword, than 'tis to make me bleed.

Let fall thy blade on vulnerable heads;

I bear a charmed life, which must not yield

To one of woman born.

Macduff

Let the angel who promised you this

Tell thee: Macduff was from his mother's womb

Untimely ripped.

Macbeth

Accursed be that tongue that tells me so.

I will not fight with thee.

Macduff

Then yield thee, coward!

Macbeth

I will not yield

To kiss the ground before young Malcolm's feet.

Though Birnam Wood be come to Dunsinane

And thou, against me, of no woman born,

Yet I will try the last. Lay on, Macduff,

And damned be him that first cries 'Hold, enough!'

They go off fighting. Malcolm, Ross and other thanes enter.

Ross

This way, my lord, the castle has been taken,

The noble thanes do bravely in the war.

The day almost declares itself as yours.

Malcolm

I would the friends we miss were safe arrived.

Ross

Some will die, my noble lord, yet even so

So great a day as this is cheaply bought.

Macduff enters with Macbeth's head.

Macduff

Hail king, for so thou art.

Behold here stands the tyrant's evil head.

All

Hail, king of Scotland! Hail, king of Scotland!

*Macduff puts down the head, takes the crown from it,
and places it on Malcolm's head.*

Malcolm

My thanes and kinsmen shall henceforth be earls,

The first that Scotland such an honour named.

Thanks be to all at once and to each one

Whom we invite to see us crowned at Scone!

TAKING THINGS FURTHER

The real read

This *Real Reads* version of *Macbeth* is a retelling of William Shakespeare's magnificent work. If you would like to read the full play in all its original splendour, many complete editions are available, from bargain paperbacks to beautifully-bound hardbacks. You should find a copy in your local bookshop or library, or even a charity shop.

Filling in the spaces

The loss of so many of William Shakespeare's original words is a sad but necessary part of the shortening process. We have had to make some difficult decisions, omitting subplots and details, some important, some less so, but all interesting. We have also, at times, taken the liberty of combining two events into one, or of giving a character words or actions that originally belong to another. The points below will fill in some of the gaps, but nothing can beat the original.

- When Macbeth arrives home to announce that Duncan, the King of Scotland, is coming to their castle, it is Lady Macbeth who suggests that they kill him to gain the crown.

- When the knocking at the south gate sends Macbeth and his wife off quickly to wash the blood from their hands and change into their nightgowns, it is the porter who goes to open the door to Macduff and Lennox. This is a short comic scene that Shakespeare puts in to give the audience something to laugh at in the middle of such a dark play.

- Macduff is sent an invitation to come to Macbeth's feast, but he ignores it, which makes Macbeth distrust him and plot to kill both him and his family.

- After the King's death, Macduff begins to suspect Macbeth and goes to England to get help from Malcolm who, as Duncan's son, should become the new King of Scotland. Malcolm isn't sure whether Macduff has been sent by Macbeth to trick him into going back so

Macbeth can kill him. Malcolm tests him to make sure he's not on Macbeth's side before agreeing to ride out with an English army to Scotland.

● Lady Macbeth slowly goes mad, and eventually kills herself.

Back in time

William Shakespeare was born in 1564 in Stratford-upon-Avon, and later went to London, where he became an actor and playwright. He was very popular in his own lifetime. He wrote thirty-seven plays that we know of, and many sonnets.

The very first theatres were built around the time that Shakespeare was growing up. Until then, plays had been performed in rooms at the back of inns or pubs. The Elizabethans loved going to watch entertainments such as bear-baiting and cock-fighting as well as plays. They also liked to watch public executions, and some of the plays written at this time were quite gruesome.

The Globe, where Shakespeare's company acted, was a round building that was open to the sky in the middle. 'Groundlings' paid a penny to stand around the stage in the central yard. They risked getting wet if it rained. Wealthier people could have a seat in the covered galleries around the edge of the space. Some very important people even had a seat on the stage itself. Unlike today's theatre-goers, Elizabethan audiences were noisy and sometimes fighting broke out.

There were no sets or scene changes in these plays. It was up to the playwright's skill with words to create thunderstorms or forests or Egyptian queens in the imagination of the audience.

Shakespeare wrote mostly in blank verse, in unrhymed lines of ten syllables with a *te-tum te-tum* rhythm. But unlike most writers of his time he tried to make his actors' lines closer to the rhythms of everyday speech, in order to make it sound more naturalistic. He used poetic imagery, and even invented words that we still use today.

His plays are mostly based on stories or old plays that he improved. *Macbeth* was inspired by a story about a real Scottish king called Macbeth, who reigned in the eleventh century. This story was told in a book called *Chronicles of England, Scotland and Ireland*, published when Shakespeare was a boy, which he used as a source for many of his history plays.

Finding out more

We recommend the following books and websites to gain a greater understanding of William Shakespeare and Elizabethan England.

Books

- Marcia Williams, *Mr William Shakespeare's Plays*, Walker Books, 2009.

- Toby Forward and Juan Wijngaard, *Shakespeare's Globe: A Pop-Up Theatre*, Walker Books, 2005.

- Alan Durband, *Shakespeare Made Easy: Macbeth*, Nelson Thornes, 1989.

- Leon Garfield, *Shakespeare Stories*, Victor Gollanz, 1985.

- Stewart Ross, *William Shakespeare*, Writers in Britain series, Evans, 1999.

- Felicity Hebditch, *Tudors*, Britain through the Ages series, Evans, 2003.

- Dereen Taylor, *The Tudors and the Stuarts*, Wayland, 2007.

Websites

- www.shakespeare.org.uk
Good general introduction to Shakespeare's life. Contains information and pictures of the houses linked to him in and around Stratford.

- www.elizabethan-era.org.uk
Lots of information including details of Elizabethan daily life.

TV and film

- *Macbeth*, RSC, 1978. Directed by Trevor Nunn.

- *Macbeth*, RSC, 1979. Directed by Philip Casson.

- *Macbeth on the Estate*, BBC TV, 1997. Directed by Penny Woolcock.

- *Shakespeare: The Animated Tales*, Metrodome Distribution Ltd, 2007.

Food for thought

Here are some things to think about if you are reading *Macbeth* alone, or ideas for discussion if you are reading it with friends.

In retelling *Macbeth* we have tried to recreate, as accurately as possible, Shakespeare's original plot and characters. We have also tried to imitate aspects of his style. Remember, however, that this is not the original work; thinking about the points below, therefore, can help you begin to understand William Shakespeare's craft.

To move forward from here, turn to the full-length version of *Macbeth* and lose yourself in his wonderful storytelling.

Starting points

- Do you think the witches deliberately tricked Macbeth with their prophecies?

- Do you think people can really tell what will happen in the future?

- What do you think might have happened if Macbeth had not murdered Duncan? How might the prophecy have come true?

- Do you think Macbeth was a strong character or a weak one? Why?

- What do you think of Lady Macbeth? What did she say was the reason for not murdering Duncan herself?

- Why do you think that Malcolm and his brother ran away when they heard that their father had been murdered?

Themes

What do you think William Shakespeare is saying about the following themes in *Macbeth*?

- ambition

- power

- belief in prophecies

Style

Can you find examples of the following?

- repetition of words for emphasis

- a simile (where something is described as being like something else)

- an iambic pentameter (see the next page)

- a rhyming couplet to show the end of a scene (see the next page)

Try your hand at writing an iambic (*eye-am-bic*) pentameter. It must have ten syllables arranged in pairs; the first syllable of each pair is unstressed and the second is stressed, like this speech by one of the Scottish lords:

The *secret murders sticking on his hands*.

Try your hand at writing a rhyming couplet, as in Macbeth's speech:

Hear it not, Duncan, for it is a *knell*
That summons thee to heaven, or to *hell*.

Something old, something new

In this *Real Reads* version of *Macbeth*, Shakespeare's original words have been interwoven with new linking text in Shakespearean style. If you are interested in knowing which words are original and which new, visit www.realreads.co.uk/shakespeare/comparison/macbeth – here you will find a version with the original words highlighted. It might be fun to guess in advance which are which!